For my mother with love. —L.M.

For Sam in Sydney, happy 4th birthday, with all my love. —M.R.

Baby Rattlesnake

Told by
Te Ata

Adapted by
Lynn Moroney

Illustrated by
Mira Reisberg

Children's Book Press, *an imprint* of Lee & Low Books Inc.
New York

Out in the place where the rattlesnakes lived,
there was a little baby rattlesnake who cried
all the time because he did not have a rattle.

He said to his mother and father, "I don't know why I don't have a rattle. I'm made just like my brother and sister. How can I be a rattlesnake if I don't have a rattle?"

Mother and Father Rattlesnake said, "You are too young to have a rattle. When you get to be as old as your brother and sister, you will have a rattle, too."

But Baby Rattlesnake did not want to wait.
So he just cried and cried.

He shook his tail and when he couldn't hear a rattle sound, he cried even louder.

Mother and Father said, "Shhh! Shhh! Shhhhh!"
Brother and Sister said, "Shhh! Shhh! Shhhhh!"

But Baby Rattlesnake wouldn't stop crying.
He kept the Rattlesnake People awake all night.

The next morning, the Rattlesnake People called a big council. They talked and they talked just like people do, but they couldn't decide how to make that little baby rattlesnake happy. He didn't want anything else but a rattle.

At last one of the elders said, "Go ahead, give him a rattle. He's just too young and he'll get into trouble. But let him learn a lesson. I just want to get some sleep."

So they gave Baby Rattlesnake a rattle.

13

Baby Rattlesnake loved his rattle. He shook his tail and for the first time he heard, "Ch-Ch-Ch! Ch-Ch-Ch!" He was so excited!

He sang a rattle song, "Ch-Ch-Ch! Ch-Ch-Ch!"

He danced a rattle dance, "Ch-Ch-Ch! Ch-Ch-Ch!"

15

Soon Baby Rattlesnake learned to play tricks with his rattle. He hid in the rocks and when small animals came by, he darted out rattling, "Ch-Ch-Ch! Ch-Ch-Ch!"

ch ch
ch ch ch

16

He made old Jack Rabbit jump.

He made Old Man Turtle jump.

He made Prairie Dog jump.

Each time Baby Rattlesnake laughed and laughed.
He thought it was fun to scare the Animal People.

Mother and Father warned Baby Rattlesnake,
"You must not use your rattle in such a way."

Big Brother and Big Sister said,
"You are not being careful with your rattle."

The Rattlesnake People told Baby Rattlesnake to
stop acting so foolish with his rattle.

Baby Rattlesnake did not listen.

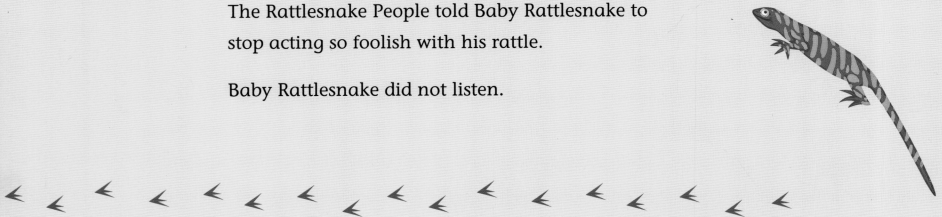

One day, Baby Rattlesnake said to his mother and father, "How will I know a chief's daughter when I see her?"

"Well, she's usually very beautiful and walks with her head held high," said Father.

"And she's very neat in her dress," added Mother.

"Why do you want to know?" asked Father.

"Because I want to scare her!" said Baby Rattlesnake.

And he started off down the path before his mother and father could warn him never to do a thing like that.

21

The little fellow reached the place where the Indians traveled.
He curled himself up on a log and he started rattling, "Ch-Ch-Ch!"
He was having a wonderful time.

All of a sudden he saw a beautiful maiden coming toward him
from a long way off. She walked with her head held high, and she
was very neat in her dress.

"Ah," thought Baby Rattlesnake. "She must be the chief's daughter."

Baby Rattlesnake hid in the rocks. He was excited.
This was going to be his best trick.

He waited and waited. The chief's daughter came closer and closer.

When she was in just the right spot, he darted out of the rocks.

"Ch-Ch-Ch-Ch-Ch!"

"HO!"

cried the chief's daughter. She whirled around, stepping on Baby Rattlesnake's rattle and crushing it to pieces.

Baby Rattlesnake looked at his beautiful rattle scattered all over the trail. He didn't know what to do.

He took off for home as fast as he could.

With great sobs, he told Mother and Father what had happened. They wiped his tears and gave him big rattlesnake hugs.

For the rest of that day, Baby Rattlesnake stayed safe and snug, close by his rattlesnake family.

ABOUT BABY RATTLESNAKE

TE ATA, whose name means "Bearer of the Morning," was an internationally acclaimed Chickasaw Indian storyteller. Born in the Oklahoma Territory in 1897, she was proclaimed Oklahoma State's first Oklahoma State treasure. She regaled audiences in the USA and Europe for over 65 years, performing at the White House during the Roosevelt years.

Oklahoma storyteller **LYNN MORONEY**, herself part Indian, had admired Te Ata for years and finally asked her permission to retell the story of Baby Rattlesnake. At first, Te Ata said no. But after hearing Lynn tell her own stories at a storytelling festival, Te Ata was so impressed that she gave Lynn her blessing to tell this story and pass it on to others as a book. She writes: "Baby Rattlesnake *is a teaching tale about what happens when you get something before you are ready for it. Subsequent to the original publication of this book, I learned that rather than being a Chickasaw story, its origin is in the oral literature of the Pawnee Nation. The traditional version of the story can be found in 'Pawnee Music' by Frances Denmore, in the Smithsonian Bureau of American Ethnology, Bulletin 93 (1929) 107-8. I am most pleased to be able to share the correct origin of this well-loved tale."*

Artist **MIRA REISBERG** fell in love with the story of *Baby Rattlesnake* the moment she heard it. Mira was born in Australia and has lived in the Southwest United States, the setting of *Baby Rattlesnake*. Her medium for this book is cut paper and gouache paints.

Special thanks to Bay Area storyteller Gay Ducey, who brought Lynn's original manuscript to Children's Book Press and then nurtured the original edition of *Baby Rattlesnake* through its completion, and to Harriet Rohmer, David Schecter, Katherine Tillotson, and Laura Chastain.

Children's Book Press, an imprint of LEE & LOW BOOKS Inc.,
95 Madison Avenue, New York, NY 10016
leeandlow.com

Manufactured in China by First Choice Printing Co. Ltd.

Book design by Andrew Ogus and Dana Goldberg
Book production by The Kids at Our House

15 14 13 12 11 10 9 8 7
Second Edition

Library of Congress Cataloging-in-Publication Data
Ata, Te.
    Baby rattlesnake / told by Te Ata; adaptation by Lynne Moroney; illustrations by Mira Reisberg = Viborita de cascabel / cuento de Te Ata; adaptación de Lynn Moroney; ilustraciones de Mira Reisberg.
        p. cm.
    Summary: Willful Baby Rattlesnake throws tantrums in order to get his rattle before he's ready, but he misuses it and learns a lesson.
    ISBN 978-0-89239-216-2 (English paperback)
1. Chickasaw Indians—Folklore. 2. Rattlesnakes—Folklore. 3. Bilingual books. [1. Chickasaw Indians—Folklore. 2. Rattlesnakes—Folklore. 3. Indians of North America—Southwest, New—Folklore. 4. Folklore—Southwest, New. 5. Spanish language materials— Bilingual.] I. Ata, Te. II. Reisberg, Mira, ill. III. Title.
    E99.C55M67 2003
    398.24'5279638'08997073—dc21
        [E]   2002041526